P9-DYJ-594

Taking Care of Mama Rabbit

ANITA LOBEL

WITHDRAWN
Anne Arundel County
Public Library

ALFRED A. KNOPF

new york

One morning, Mama Rabbit stayed in bed.
That made her ten little rabbits worried.

"Where is Papa?" they asked.

"Papa went to get me medicine," Mama
mumbled.

Medicine!
Mama did look very pale.
And not at all happy.

"We have to cheer up Mama," the ten little
rabbits agreed.
One by one, they brought her:

A fresh handkerchief.

A delicious cookie.

A juicy apple.

A cuddly toy.

A steaming cup of hot chocolate.

A sweet-smelling flower.

A pretty ribbon.

A shiny necklace.

A colorful picture.

A good book.

Mama Rabbit looked much happier.
And not so pale anymore.

"Now we have a special surprise for you, Mama!"
the ten little rabbits said.

Just then, Papa Rabbit walked through the door.
"I have brought your medicine, dear," he said.

Mama hopped out of bed.

"Thank you, Papa," she said.

"But I don't really think I need medicine.
Our darling rabbits have made me all better
without it."

Mama hopped out of bed.
"Thank you, Papa," she said.
"But I don't really think I need medicine.
Our darling rabbits have made me all better
without it."

THIS IS A BORZOI BOOK PUBLISHED BY ALFRED A. KNOPF

Copyright © 2014 by Anita Lobel

All rights reserved. Published in the United States by Alfred A. Knopf, an imprint of Random House Children's Books, a division of Random House, Inc., New York.

Knopf, Borzoi Books, and the colophon are registered trademarks of Random House, Inc.

Visit us on the Web! randomhouse.com/kids

Educators and librarians, for a variety of teaching tools, visit us at RHTeachersLibrarians.com

Library of Congress Cataloging-in-Publication Data
Lobel, Anita.
Taking care of Mama Rabbit / Anita Lobel. — First edition.
p. cm.
Summary: "When Mama Rabbit falls ill, her ten little rabbits each tend to her in their own way." — Provided by publisher
ISBN 978-0-385-75368-5 (trade) — ISBN 978-0-385-75369-2 (lib. bdg.) — ISBN 978-0-385-75370-8 (ebook)
[1. Mother and child—Fiction. 2. Sick—Fiction. 3. Rabbits—Fiction.] I. Title.
PZ7.L7794Tak 2014
[E]—dc23
2013003154

The text of this book is set in 16-point Bookman Old Style.
The illustrations were created using gouache and watercolor.

MANUFACTURED IN MALAYSIA
February 2014
10 9 8 7 6 5 4 3 2 1

First Edition

Random House Children's Books supports the First Amendment and celebrates the right to read.

The ten little rabbits lined up and put on a show for their mama and papa.

Mama and Papa Rabbit clapped and cried, "Bravo, bravo! We have the nicest, sweetest, cleverest little rabbits in the whole world."